I0823672

THE
HAUNTED BOOKSHELF

he telling or reading of ghost stories during long, dark, and cold Christmas nights is a yuletide ritual dating back to at least the eighteenth century, and was once as much a part of Christmas tradition as decorating fir trees, feasting on goose, and the singing of carols. During the Victorian era many magazines printed ghost stories specifically for the Christmas season. These "winter tales" didn't necessarily explore Christmas themes. Rather, they were offered as an eerie pleasure to be enjoyed on Christmas Eve with the family, adding a supernatural shiver to the seasonal chill.

The tradition remained strong in the British Isles (and her colonies) throughout much of the twentieth century, though in recent years it has been on the wane. Certainly, few people in Canada or the United States seem to know about it any longer. This series of small books seeks to rectify this, to revive a charming custom for the long, dark nights we all know so well here at Christmastime.

Charles Dickens
The Signalman

A.M. Burrage
One Who Saw

Edith Wharton
Afterward

M.R. James
The Diary of Mr. Poynter

Marjorie Bowen
The Crown Derby Plate

E.F. Benson
How Fear Departed the Long Gallery

W.W. Jacobs
The Toll House

Algernon Blackwood
The Empty House

H. Russell Wakefield
The Red Lodge

Frank Cowper
Christmas Eve on a Haunted Hulk

R.H. Malden
The Sundial

Elizabeth Gaskell
The Old Nurse's Story

Daphne du Maurier
The Apple Tree

Richard Bridgeman
The Morgan Trust

M.R. James
The Story of a Disappearance and an Appearance

Walter de la Mare
The Green Room

Margaret Oliphant
The Open Door

Bernard Capes
An Eddy on the Floor

F. Marion Crawford
The Doll's Ghost

Edith Wharton
Mr. Jones

Shirley Jackson
A Visit

Cynthia Asquith
The Corner Shop

Gertrude Atherton
The Dead and the Countess

Arthur Conan Doyle
The Captain of the Polestar

Marjorie Bowen
The House by the Poppy Field

Andrew Caldecott
A Room in a Rectory

L.P. Hartley
Podolo

Laurence Whistler
Captain Dalgety Returns

Mary Fitt
The Amethyst Cross

Rosemary Timperley
The Mistress in Black

Sarah Orne Jewett
Lady Ferry

H. Russell Wakefield
Lucky's Grove

LADY FERRY

REQUIESCAT
· IN PACE ·

LADY FERRY

SARAH ORNE JEWETT

A GHOST STORY FOR CHRISTMAS

DESIGNED & DECORATED BY SETH

BIBLIOASIS

E HAVE AN instinctive fear of death, yet we have a horror of a life prolonged far beyond the average limit: it is sorrowful; it is pitiful; it has no attractions.

This world is only a schoolroom for the larger life of the next. Some leave it early, and some late: some linger long after they seem to have learned all its lessons. This world is no heaven: its pleasures do not last even through our little lifetimes.

There are many fables of endless life, which in all ages have caught the attention of men; we are familiar with the stories of the old patriarchs who lived their hundreds of years, but one thinks of them wearily, and without envy.

* * *

WHEN I WAS a child, it was necessary that my father and mother should take a long sea voyage. I had never been separated from them before; but at this time they thought it best to leave me behind, as I was not strong, and the life on board a ship did not suit me. When I was told of this decision, I was very sorry, and at once thought I should be miserable without my mother; besides, I pitied myself exceedingly for losing the sights I had hoped to see in the country which they were to visit. I had an uncontrollable dislike to being sent to school, having in some way been frightened by a maid of my mother's, who had put many ideas and aversions into my head which I was many years in outgrowing. Having dreaded this possibility, it was a great relief to know that I was not to be sent to school at all, but to be put under the charge of two elderly cousins of my father—a gentleman and his wife whom I had once seen, and liked dearly. I knew that their home was at a fine old-fashioned country place, far from town, and close beside a river, and I was pleased with this prospect, and at once began to make charming plans for the new life.

I had lived always with grown people, and seldom had anything to do with children. I was very small for my age, and a strange mixture of childishness and maturity; and, having the appearance of being absorbed in my own affairs, no one ever noticed me much, or seemed to think it better that I should not listen to the conversation. In spite of considerable curiosity, I followed an instinct which directed me never to ask questions at these times: so I often heard stray sentences which puzzled me, and which really would have been made simple and commonplace at once, if I had only asked their meaning. I was, for most of the time, in a world of my own. I had a great deal of imagination, and was always telling myself stories; and my mind was adrift in these so much, that my real absentmindedness was mistaken for childish unconcern. Yet I was a thoroughly simple, unaffected child. My dreams and thoughtfulness gave me a certain tact and perception unusual in a child; but my pleasures were as deep in simple things as the heart could wish.

It happened that our cousin Matthew was to come to the city on business the week that the ship was to sail, and that I could stay with my father and mother to the very last day, and then go home with him. This was much pleasanter than leaving sooner under the care of an utter stranger, as was at first planned. My cousin Agnes wrote a kind letter about my coming which seemed to give her much pleasure. She remembered me very well, and sent me a message which made me feel of consequence; and I was delighted with the plan of making her so long a visit.

One evening I was reading a storybook, and I heard my father say in an undertone, "How long has madam been at the ferry this last time? Eight or ten years, has she not? I suppose she is there yet?"—"Oh, yes!" said my mother, "or Agnes would have told us. She spoke of her in the last letter you had, while we were in Sweden."

"I should think she would be glad to have a home at last, after her years of wandering about. Not that I should be surprised now to hear that she had disappeared again. When I was staying there while I was young, we thought she had drowned herself, and even had the men search for her along the shore of the river; but after a time cousin Matthew heard of her alive and well in Salem; and I believe she appeared again this last time as suddenly as she went away."

"I suppose she will never die," said my mother gravely. "She must be terribly old," said my father. "When I saw her last, she had scarcely changed at all from the way she looked when I was a boy. She is even more quiet and gentle than she used to be. There is no danger that the child will have any fear of her; do you think so?"—"Oh, no! But I think I will tell her that madam is a very old woman, and that I hope she will be very kind, and try not to annoy her; and that she must not be frightened at her strange notions. I doubt if she knows what craziness is."—"She would be wise if she could define it," said my father with a smile. "Perhaps we had better say nothing about the old lady. It is probable that she stays altogether in her own room, and that the child will rarely see her. I have never realized until lately the horror of such a long life as hers, living on and on, with one's friends gone long ago: such an endless life in this world!"

Then there was a mysterious old person living at the ferry, and there was a question whether I would not be "afraid" of her. She "had not changed" since my father was a boy: "it was horrible to have one's life endless in this world!"

The days went quickly by. My mother, who was somewhat of an invalid, grew sad as the time drew near for saying good-bye to me, and was more tender and kind than ever before, and more indulgent of every wish and fancy of mine. We had been together all my life, and now it was to be long months before she could possibly see my face again, and perhaps she was leaving me forever. Her time was all spent, I believe, in thoughts for me, and in making arrangements for my comfort. I did see my mother again; the tears fill my eyes when I think how dear we became to each other before that first parting, and with what a lingering, loving touch, she herself packed my boxes, and made sure, over and over again, that I had whatever I should need; and I remember how close she used to hold me when I sat in her lap in the evening, saying that she was afraid I should have grown too large to be held when she came back again. We had more to say to each other than ever before, and I think, until then, that my mother never had suspected how much I observed of life and of older people in a certain way; that I was something more than a little child who went from one interest to another carelessly. I have known since that my mother's childhood was much like mine. She, however, was timid, while I had inherited from my father his fearlessness and lack of suspicion; and these qualities, like a fresh wind, swept away any cobwebs of nervous anticipation and sensitiveness. Everyone was kind to me, partly, I think, because I interfered with no one. I was glad of the kindness, and, with my unsuspected dreaming and my happy childishness, I had gone through life with almost perfect contentment, until this pain of my first real loneliness came into my heart.

It was a day's journey to cousin Matthew's house, mostly by rail; though, toward the end, we had to travel a considerable distance by stage, and at last were left on the riverbank opposite my new home, and I saw a boat waiting to take us across. It was just at sunset, and I remember wondering if my father and mother were out of sight of land, and if they were watching the sky; if my father would remember that only the evening before we had gone out for a walk together, and there had been a sunset so much like this. It somehow seemed long ago. Cousin Matthew was busy talking with the ferryman; and indeed he had found acquaintances at almost every part of the journey, and had not been much with me, though he was kind and attentive in his courteous, old-fashioned way, treating me with the same ceremonious politeness which he had shown my mother. He pointed out the house to me: it was but a little way from the edge of the river. It was very large and irregular, with great white chimneys; and, while the river was all in shadow, the upper windows of two high gables were catching the last red glow of the sun. On the opposite side of a green from the house were the farmhouse and buildings; and the green sloped down to the water, where there was a wharf and an ancient-looking storehouse. There were some old boats and long sticks of timber lying on the shore; and I saw a flock of white geese march solemnly up toward the barns. From the open green I could see that a road went up the hill beyond. The trees in the garden and orchard were the richest green; their round tops were clustered thick together; and there were some royal great elms near the house. The fiery red faded from the high windows as we came near the shore, and cousin Agnes was ready to meet me; and when she put her arms round me as kindly as my mother would have done, and kissed me twice in my father's fashion, I was sure that I loved her, and would be contented.

Her hair was very grey; but she did not look, after all, so very old. Her face was a grave one, as if she had had many cares; yet they had all made her stronger, and there had been some sweetness, and something to be glad about, and to thank God for, in every sorrow. I had a feeling always that she was my sure defence and guard. I was safe and comfortable with her: it was the same feeling which one learns to have toward God more and more, as one grows older.

We went in through a wide hall, and upstairs, through a long passage, to my room, which was in a corner of one of the gables. Two windows looked on the garden and the river: another looked across to the other gable, and into the square, grassy court between. It was a rambling, great house, and seemed like some English houses I had seen. It would be great fun to go into all the rooms someday soon.

"How much you are like your father!" said cousin Agnes, stooping to kiss me again, with her hand on my shoulder. I had a sudden consciousness of my bravery in having behaved so well all day; then I remembered that my father and mother were at every instant being carried farther and farther away. I could almost hear the waves dash about the ship; and I could not help crying a little. "Poor little girl!" said cousin Agnes. "I am very sorry." And she sat down, and took me in her lap for a few minutes. She was tall, and held me so comfortably, and I soon was almost happy again; for she hoped I would not be lonely with her, and that I would not think she was a stranger, for she had known and loved my father so well; and it would make cousin Matthew so disappointed and uneasy if I were discontented; and would I like some bread and milk with my supper, in the same blue china bowl, with the dragon on it, which my father used to have when he was a boy? These arguments were by no means lost upon me, and I was ready to smile presently; and then we went down to the dining room, which had some solemn-looking portraits on the walls, and heavy, stiff furniture; and there was an old-fashioned woman standing ready to wait, whom cousin Agnes called Deborah, and who smiled at me graciously.

Cousin Matthew talked with his wife for a time about what had happened to him and to her during his absence; and then he said, "And how is madam today? You have not spoken of her."—"She is not so well as usual," said cousin Agnes. "She has had one of her sorrowful times since you went away. I have sat with her for several hours today, but she has hardly spoken to me." And then cousin Matthew looked at me, and cousin Agnes hesitated for a minute. Deborah had left the room.

"We speak of a member of our family whom you have not seen, although you may have heard your father speak of her. She is called Lady Ferry by most people who know of her; but you may say madam when you speak to her. She is very old, and her mind wanders, so that she has many strange fancies; but you must not be afraid, for she is very gentle and harmless. She is not used to children; but I know you will not annoy her, and I dare say you can give her much pleasure." This was all that was said; but I wished to know more. It seemed to me that there was a reserve about this person, and the old house itself was the very place for a mystery. As I went through some of the other rooms with cousin Agnes in the summer twilight, I half expected to meet Lady Ferry in every shadowy corner; but I did not dare to ask a question. My father's words came to me—"Such an endless life," and "living on and on." And why had he and my mother never spoken to me afterward of my seeing her? They had talked about it again, perhaps, and did not mean to tell me, after all.

I saw something of the house that night, the great kitchen, with its huge fireplace, and other rooms up stairs and down; and cousin Agnes told me that by daylight I should go everywhere, except to Madam's rooms: I must wait for an invitation there.

The house had been built a hundred and fifty years before, by Colonel Haverford, an Englishman, whom no one knew much about, except that he lived like a prince, and would never tell his history. He and his sons died; and after the revolution the house was used for a tavern for many years—the Ferry Tavern—and the place was busy enough.

Then there was a bridge built down the river, and the old ferry fell into disuse; and the owner of the house died, and his family also died, or went away; and then the old place, for a long time, was either vacant, or in the hands of different owners. It was going to ruin at length, when cousin Matthew bought it, and came there from the city to live years before. He was a strange man; indeed, I know now that all the possessors of the Ferry farm must have been strange men. One often hears of the influence of climate upon character; there is a strong influence of place; and the inanimate things which surround us indoors and out make us follow out in our lives their own silent characteristics. We unconsciously catch the tone of every house in which we live, and of every view of the outward, material world which grows familiar to us, and we are influenced by surroundings nearer and closer still than the climate or the country which we inhabit. At the old Haverford house, it was mystery which one felt when one entered the door; and when one came away, after cordiality, and days of sunshine and pleasant hospitality, it was still with a sense of this mystery, and of something unseen and unexplained. Not that there was any thing covered and hidden necessarily; but it was the quiet undertone in the house which had grown to be so old, and had known the magnificent living of Colonel Haverford's time, and afterward the struggles of poor gentlemen and women, who had hardly warmed its walls with their pitiful fires, and shivering, hungry lives; then the long procession of travellers who had been sheltered there in its old tavern days; finally, my cousin Matthew and his wife, who had made it their home, when, with all their fortune, they felt empty-handed, and as if their lives were ended, because their only son had died. Here they had learned to be happy again in a quiet sort of way, and had become older and serener, loving this lovable place by the river, and keepers of its secret—whatever that might be.

I was wide awake that first evening: I was afraid of being sent to bed, and, to show cousin Agnes that I was not sleepy, I chattered far more than usual. It was warm, and the windows of the parlor where we sat looked upon the garden. The moon had risen, and it was light out of doors. I caught every now and then the faint smell of honeysuckle, and presently I asked if I might go into the garden awhile; and cousin Agnes gave me leave, adding that I must soon go to bed, else I would be very tired the next day. She noticed that I looked grave, and said that I must not dread being alone in the strange room, for it was so near her own. This was a great consolation; and after I had been told that the tide was in, and I must be careful not to go too near the river wall, I went out through the tall glass door, and slowly down the wide garden walk, from which now and then narrower walks branched off at right angles. It was the pride of the place, this garden; and the box borders especially were kept with great care. They had partly been trimmed that day; and the evening dampness brought out the faint, solemn odor of the leaves, which I never have noticed since without thinking of that night. The roses were in bloom, and the snowball bushes were startlingly white, and there was a long border filled with lilies-of-the-valley. The other flowers of the season were all there and in blossom; yet I could see none well but the white ones, which looked like bits of snow and ice in the summer shadows—ghostly flowers which one could see at night.

It was still in the garden, except once I heard a bird twitter sleepily, and once or twice a breeze came across the river, rustling the leaves a little. The small-paned windows glistened in the moonlight, and seemed like the eyes of the house watching me, the unknown newcomer.

For a while I wandered about, exploring the different paths, some of which were arched over by the tall lilacs, or by arbors where the grape leaves did not seem fully grown. I wondered if my mother would miss me. It seemed impossible that I should have seen her only that morning; and suddenly I had a consciousness that she was thinking of me, and she seemed so close to me, that it would not be strange if she could hear what I said. And I called her twice softly; but the sound of my unanswered voice frightened me. I saw some round white flowers at my feet, looking up mockingly.

The smell of the earth and the new grass seemed to smother me. I was afraid to be there all alone in the wide open air; and all the tall bushes that were so still around me took strange shapes, and seemed to be alive. I was so terribly far away from the mother whom I had called; the pleasure of my journey, and my coming to cousin Agnes, faded from my mind, and that indescribable feeling of hopelessness and dread, and of having made an irreparable mistake, came in its place. The thorns of a straying, slender branch of a rose bush caught my sleeve maliciously as I turned to hurry away, and then I caught sight of a person in the path just before me. It was such a relief to see someone, that I was not frightened when I saw that it must be Lady Ferry.

She was bent, but very tall and slender, and was walking slowly with a cane. Her head was covered with a great hood or wrapping of some kind, which she pushed back when she saw me. Some faint whitish figures on her dress looked like frost in the moonlight; and the dress itself was made of some strange stiff silk, which rustled softly like dry rushes and grasses in the autumn—a rustling noise that carries a chill with it. She came close to me, a sorrowful little figure very dreary at heart, standing still as the flowers themselves; and for several minutes she did not speak, but watched me, until I began to be afraid of her. Then she held out her hand, which trembled as if it were trying to shake off its rings. "My dear," said she, "I bid you welcome: I have known your father. I was told of your coming. Perhaps you will walk with me? I did not think to find you here alone." There was a fascinating sweetness in Madam's voice, and I at once turned to walk beside her, holding her hand fast, and keeping pace

with her feeble steps. "Then you are not afraid of me?" asked the old lady, with a strange quiver in her voice. "It is a long time since I have seen a child."—"No," said I, "I am not afraid of you. I was frightened before I saw you, because I was all alone, and I wished I could see my father and mother." And I hung my head so that my new friend could not see the tears in my eyes, for she watched me curiously. "All alone: that is like me," said she to herself. "All alone? A child is not all alone, but there is no one like me. I am something alone: there is nothing else of my fashion, a creature who lives forever!" and Lady Ferry sighed pitifully. Did she mean that she never was going to die like other people? But she was silent, and I did not dare to ask for any explanation as we walked back and forward. Her fingers kept moving round my wrist, smoothing it as if she liked to feel it, and to keep my hand in hers. It seemed to give her pleasure to have me with her, and I felt quite at my ease presently, and began to talk a little, assuring her that I did not mind having taken the journey of that day. I had taken some long journeys: I had been to China once, and it took a great while to get there; but London was the nicest place I had ever seen; had Lady Ferry ever been in London? And I was surprised to hear her say drearily that she had been in London; she had been everywhere.

"Did you go to Westminster Abbey?" I asked, going on with the conversation childishly. "And did you see where Queen Elizabeth and Mary Queen of Scots are buried? Mamma had told me all about them."

"Buried, did you say? Are they dead too?" asked Madam eagerly. "Yes, indeed!" said I. "They have been dead a long time."—"Ah! I had forgotten," answered my strange companion. "Do you know of anyone else who has died beside them? I have not heard of anyone's dying and going home for so long! Once everyone died but me—except some young people; and I do not know them."—"Why, everyone must die," said I, wonderingly. "There is a funeral somewhere every day, I suppose."—"Everyone but me," Madam repeated sadly, "everyone but me, and I am alone."

Just now cousin Agnes came to the door, and called me. "Go in now, child," said Lady Ferry. "You may come and sit with me tomorrow if you choose." And I said goodnight, while she turned, and went down the walk with feeble, lingering steps. She paced to and fro, as I often saw her afterwards, on the flagstones; and some bats flew that way like ragged bits of darkness, holding somehow a spark of life. I watched her for a minute: she was like a ghost, I thought, but not a fearful ghost—poor Lady Ferry!

"Have you had a pleasant walk?" asked cousin Matthew politely. "Tomorrow, I will give you a border for your own, and some plants for it, if you like gardening." I joyfully answered that I should like it very much, and so I began to feel already the pleasure of being in a real home, after the wandering life to which I had become used. I went close to cousin Agnes's chair to tell her confidentially that I had been walking with Madam in the garden, and she was very good to me, and asked me to come to sit with her the next day; but she said very odd things.

"You must not mind what she says," said cousin Agnes; "and I would never dispute with her, or even seem surprised, if I were you. It hurts and annoys her, and she soon forgets her strange fancies. I think you seem a very sensible little girl, and I have told you about this poor friend of ours as if you were older. But you understand, do you not?" And then she kissed me good-night, and I went upstairs, contented with her assurance that she would come to me before I went to sleep.

I found a pleasant-faced young girl busy putting away some of my clothing. I had seen her just after supper, and had fancied her very much, partly because she was not so old as the rest of the servants. We were friendly at once, and I found her very talkative; so finally I asked the question which was uppermost in my mind—Did she know anything about Madam?

"Lady Ferry, folks call her," said Martha, much interested. "I never have seen her close to, only from the other side of the garden, where she walks at night. She never goes out by day. Deborah waits upon her. I haven't been here long; but I have always heard about Madam, bless you! Folks tell all kinds of strange stories. She's fearful old, and there's many believes she never will die; and where she came from nobody knows. I've heard that her folks used to live here; but nobody can remember them, and she used to wander about; and once before she was here—a good while ago; but this last time she come was nine years ago; one stormy night she came across the ferry, and scared them to death, looking in at the window like a ghost. She said she used to live here in Colonel Haverford's time. They saw she wasn't right in her head—the ferrymen did. But she came up to the house, and they let her in, and she went straight to the rooms in the north gable, and she never has gone away; it was in an awful storm she come, I've heard, and she looked just the same as she does now. There! I can't tell half the stories I've heard, and Deborah she most took my head off," said Martha, "because, when I first came, I was asking about her; and she said it was a sin to gossip about a harmless old creature whose mind was broke, but I guess most everybody thinks there's something mysterious. There's my grandmother—her mind is failing her; but she never had such ways! And then those clothes that my lady in the gable wears: they're unearthly looking; and I heard a woman say once, that they come out of a chest in the big garret, and they belonged to a Mistress Haverford who was hung for a witch, but there's no knowing that there is any truth in it." And Martha would have gone on with her stories, if just then we had not heard cousin Agnes's step on the stairway, and I hurried to bed.

But my bright eyes and excited look betrayed me. Cousin Agnes said she had hoped I would be asleep. And Martha said perhaps it was her fault; but I seemed wakeful, and she had talked with me a bit, to keep my spirits up, coming to a new, strange place. The apology was accepted, but Martha evidently had orders before I next saw her; for I never could get her to discuss Lady Ferry again; and she carefully told me that she should not have told those foolish stories, which were not true: but I knew that she still had her thoughts and suspicions as well as I. Once, when I asked her if Lady Ferry were Madam's real name, she answered with a guilty flush, "That's what the folks hereabout called her, because they didn't know any other at first." And this to me was another mystery. It was strongly impressed upon my mind that I must ask no questions, and that Madam was not to be discussed. No one distinctly forbade this; but I felt that it would not do. In every other way I was sure that I was allowed perfect liberty, so I soon ceased to puzzle myself or other people, and accepted Madam's presence as being perfectly explainable and natural—just as the rest of the household did—except once in a while something would set me at work romancing and wondering; and I read some stories in one of the books in the library—of Peter Rugg, the missing man, whom one may always meet riding from Salem to Boston in every storm, and of the Flying Dutchman, and the Wandering Jew, and some terrible German stories of doomed people, and curses that were fulfilled. These made a great impression upon me; still, I was not afraid, for all such things were far outside the boundaries of my safe little world; and I played by myself along the shore of the river and in the garden; and I had my lessons with cousin Agnes, and drives with cousin Matthew who was nearly always silent, but very kind to me. The house itself was an unfailing entertainment, with its many rooms, most of which were never occupied, and its quaint, sober furnishings, some of which were as old as the house itself. It was like a storybook; and no one minded my going where I pleased.

I missed my father and mother; but the only time I was really unhappy was the first morning after my arrival. Cousin Agnes was ill with a severe headache; cousin Matthew had ridden away to attend to some business; and, being left to myself, I had a most decided reaction from my unnaturally bright feelings of the day before. I began to write a letter to my mother; but unluckily I knew how many weeks must pass before she saw it, and it was useless to try to go on. I was lonely and homesick. The rain fell heavily, and the garden looked forlorn, and so unlike the enchanting moonlighted place where I had been in the evening! The walks were like little canals; and the rose bushes looked wet and chilly, like some gay young lady who had been caught in the rain in her party dress. It was low tide in the middle of the day, and the river flats looked dismal. I fed cousin Agnes's flock of tame sparrows which came around the windows, and afterward some robins. I found some books and some candy which had come in my trunk, but my heart was very sad; and just after noon I was overjoyed when one of the servants told me that cousin Agnes would like to have me come to her room.

She was even kinder to me than she had been the night before; but she looked very ill, and at first I felt awkward, and did not know what to say. "I am afraid you have been very dull, dearie," said she, reaching out her hand to me. "I am sorry, and my headache hardly lets me think at all yet. But we will have better times tomorrow—both of us. You must ask for what you want;

and you may come and spend this evening with me, for I shall be getting well then. It does me good to see your kind little face. Suppose you make Madam a call this afternoon. She told me last night that she wished for you, and I was so glad. Deborah will show you the way."

Deborah talked to me softly, out of deference to her mistress's headache, as we went along the crooked passages. "Don't you mind what Madam says, leastways don't you dispute her. She's got a funeral going on today;" and the grave woman smiled grimly at me. "It's curious she's taken to you so; for she never will see any strange folks. Nobody speaks to her about new folks lately," she added warningly, as she tapped at the door, and Madam asked, "Is it the child?" And Deborah lifted the latch. When I was fairly inside, my interest in life came back redoubled, and I was no longer sad, but looked round eagerly. Madam spoke to me, with her sweet old voice, in her courtly, quiet way, and stood looking out of the window.

There were two tall chests of drawers in the room, with shining brass handles and ornaments; and at one side, near the door, was a heavy mahogany table, on which I saw a large leather-covered Bible, a decanter of wine and some glasses, beside some cakes in a queer old tray. And there was no other furniture but a great number of chairs which seemed to have been collected from different parts of the house.

With these the room was almost filled, except an open space in the centre, toward which they all faced. One window was darkened; but Madam had pushed back the shutter of the other, and stood looking down at the garden. I waited for her to speak again after the first salutation, and presently she said I might be seated; and I took the nearest chair, and again waited her pleasure. It was gloomy enough, with the silence and the twilight in the room; and the rain and wind out of doors sounded louder than they had in cousin Agnes's room; but soon Lady Ferry came toward me.

"So you did not forget the old woman," said she, with a strange emphasis on the word old, as if that were her title and her chief characteristic. "And were not you afraid? I am glad it seemed worthwhile; for tomorrow would have been too late. You may like to remember by and by that you came. And my funeral is to be tomorrow, at last. You see the room is in readiness. You will care to be here, I hope. I would have ordered you some gloves if I had known; but these are all too large for your little hands. You shall have a ring; I will leave a command for that." And Madam seated herself near me in a curious, high-backed chair. She was dressed that day in a maroon brocade, figured with bunches of dim pink flowers; and some of these flowers looked to me like wicked little faces. It was a mocking, silly creature that I saw at the side of every prim bouquet, and I looked at the faded little imps, until they seemed as much alive as Lady Ferry herself.

Her head nodded continually, as if it were keeping time to an inaudible tune, as she sat there stiffly erect. Her skin was pale and withered; and her cheeks were wrinkled in fine lines, like the crossings of a cobweb. Her eyes might once have been blue; but they had become nearly colourless, and, looking at her, one might easily imagine that she was blind. She had a singularly sweet smile, and a musical voice, which, though sad, had no trace of whining. If it had not been for her smile and her voice, I think Madam would have been a terror to me.

I noticed today, for the first time, a curious fragrance, which seemed to come from her old brocades and silks. It was very sweet, but unlike anything I had ever known before; and it was by reason of this that afterward I often knew, with a little flutter at my heart, she had been in some other rooms of the great house beside her own. This perfume seemed to linger for a little while wherever she had been, and yet it was so faint! I used to go into the darkened chambers often, or even stay for a while by myself in the unoccupied lower rooms, and I would find this fragrance, and wonder if she were one of the oldtime fairies, who could vanish at their own will and pleasure, and wonder, too, why she had come to the room. But I never met her at all.

That first visit to her and the strange fancy she had about the funeral I have always remembered distinctly.

"I am glad you came," Madam repeated. "I was finding the day long. I am all ready, you see. I shall place a little chair which is in the next room, beside your cousin's seat for you. Mrs Agnes is ill, I hear; but I think she will come tomorrow. Have you heard anyone say if many guests are expected?"— "No, Madam," I answered, "no one has told me;" and just then the thought flitted through my head that she had said the evening before that all her friends were gone. Perhaps she expected their ghosts: that would not be stranger than all the rest.

The open space where Lady Ferry had left room for her coffin began to be a horror to me, and I wished Deborah would come back, or that my hostess would open the shutters; and it was a great relief when she rose and went into the adjoining room, bidding me follow her, and there opened a drawer containing some old jewelry;

there were also some queer Chinese carvings, yellow with age—just the things a child would enjoy. I looked at them delightedly. This was coming back to more familiar life; and I soon felt more at ease, and chattered to Lady Ferry of my own possessions, and some coveted treasures of my mother's, which were to be mine when I grew older.

Madam stood beside me patiently, and listened with a half smile to my whispered admiration. In the clearer light I could see her better, and she seemed older—so old, so old! And my father's words came to me again. She had not changed since he was a boy; living on and on, and "the horror of an endless life in this world!" And I remembered what Martha had said to me, and the consciousness of this mystery was a great weight upon me all of a sudden. Why was she living so long? And what had happened to her? And how long could it be since she was a child?

There was something in her manner which made me behave, even in my pleasure, as if her imagined funeral were there in reality, and as if, in spite of my being amused and tearless, the solemn company of funeral guests already sat in the next room to us with bowed heads, and all the shadows in the world had assembled there materialized into the tangible form of crape. I opened and closed the boxes gently, and, when I had seen everything, I looked up with a sigh to think that such a pleasure was ended, and asked if I might see them again someday. But the look in her face made me recollect myself, and my own grew crimson, for it seemed at that moment as real to me as to Lady Ferry herself that this was her last day of mortal life. She walked away, but presently came back, while I was wondering if I might not go, and opened the drawer again. It creaked, and the brass handles clacked in a startling way, and she took out a little case, and said I might keep it to remember her by. It held a little vinaigrette—a tiny silver box with a gold one inside, in which I found a bit of fine sponge, dark brown with age, and still giving a faint, musty perfume and spiciness. The outside was rudely chased, and was worn as if it had been carried for years in somebody's pocket. It had a spring, the secret of which Lady Ferry showed me. I was delighted, and instinctively lifted my face to kiss her. She bent over me, and waited an instant for me to kiss her again. "Oh!" said she, softly, "it is so long since a child has kissed me! I pray God not to leave you lingering like me, apart from all your kindred, and your life so long that you forget you ever were a child."—"I will kiss you every day," said I, and then again remembered that there were to be no more days according to her plan; but she did not seem to notice my mistake.

And after this I used to go to see Madam often. For a time there was always the same gloom and hushed way of speaking, and the funeral services were to be on the morrow; but at last one day I found Deborah sedately putting the room in order, and Lady Ferry apologized for its being in such confusion; the idea of the funeral had utterly vanished, and I hurried to tell cousin Agnes with great satisfaction. I think that both she and cousin Matthew had a dislike for my being too much with Madam. I was kept out of doors as much as possible because it was much better for my health; and through the long summer days I strayed about wherever I chose. The country life was new and delightful to me. At home,

Lady Ferry's vagaries were carelessly spoken of, and often smiled at; but I gained the idea that they disguised the truth, and were afraid of my being frightened. She often talked about persons who had been dead a very long time, familiar characters in history, and, though cousin Agnes had said that she used to be fond of reading, it seemed to me that Madam might have known these men and women after all.

Once a middle-aged gentleman, an acquaintance of cousin Matthew's, came to pass a day and night at the ferry, and something happened then which seemed wonderful to me. It was early in the evening after tea, and we were in the parlor; from my seat by cousin Agnes, I could look out into the garden, and presently, with the gathering darkness, came Lady Ferry, silent as a shadow herself, to walk to and fro on the flagstones. The windows were all open, and the guest had a clear, loud voice, and pleasant, hearty laugh; and, as he talked earnestly with cousin Matthew, I noticed that Lady Ferry stood still, as if she were listening. Then I was attracted by some story which was being told, and forgot her, but afterward turned with a start, feeling that there was someone watching; and, to my astonishment, Madam had come to the long window by which one went out to the garden. She stood there a moment, looking puzzled and wild; then she smiled, and, entering, walked in most stately fashion down the long room, toward the gentlemen, before whom she courtesied with great elegance, while the stranger stopped speaking, and looked at her with amazement, as he rose, and returned her greeting.

"My dear Captain Jack McAllister!" said she. "What a surprise! And are you not home soon from your voyage? This is indeed a pleasure." And Lady Ferry seated herself, motioning to him to take the chair beside her. She looked younger than I had ever seen her; a bright colour came into her cheeks; and she talked so gayly, in such a different manner from her usual mournful gentleness. She must have been a beautiful woman; indeed she was that still.

"And did the good ship *Starlight* make a prosperous voyage? And had you many perils? Do you bring much news to us from the Spanish Main? We have missed you sadly at the assemblies; but there must be a dance in your honour. And your wife; is she not overjoyed at the sight of you? I think you have grown old and sedate since you went away. You do not look the gay sailor, or seem so light-hearted."

"I do not understand you, madam," said the stranger. "I am certainly John McAllister; but I am no captain, neither have I been at sea. Good God! Is it my grandfather whom you confuse me with?" cried he. "He was Jack McAllister, and was lost at sea more than seventy years ago, while my own father was a baby. I am told that I am wonderfully like his portrait; but he was a younger man than I when he died. This is some masquerade."

Lady Ferry looked at him intently, but the light in her face was fast fading out. "Lost at sea—lost at sea, were you, Jack McAllister, seventy years ago? I know nothing of years; one of my days is like another, and they are grey days, they creep away and hide, and sometimes one comes back to mock me. I have lived a thousand years; do you know it? Lost at sea—captain of the ship *Starlight*? Whom did you say?—Jack McAllister, yes, I knew him well—pardon me; good evening." And my lady rose, and with her head nodding and drooping, with a sorrowful, hunted look in her eyes, went out again into the shadows. She had had a flash of youth, the candle had blazed up brilliantly; but it went out again as suddenly, with flickering and smoke.

"I was startled when I saw her beside me," said Mr McAllister. "Pray, who is she? She is like no one I have ever seen. I have been told that I am like my grandfather in looks and in voice; but it is years since I have seen anyone who knew him well. And did you hear her speak of dancing? It is like seeing one who has risen from the dead. How old can she be?"—"I do not know," said cousin Matthew, "one can only guess at her age."—"Would not she come back? I should like to question her," asked the other. But cousin Matthew answered that she always refused to see strangers, and it would be no use to urge her, she would not answer him.

"Who is she? Is she any kin of yours?" asked Mr McAllister.

"Oh, no!" said my cousin Agnes. "She has had no relatives since I have known her, and I think she has no friends now but ourselves. She has been with us a long time, and once before this house was her home for a time—many years since. I suppose no one will ever know the whole history of her life; I wish often that she had power to tell it. We are glad to give shelter, and the little care she will accept, to the poor soul, God only knows where she has strayed and what she has seen. It is an enormous burden—so long a life, and such a weight of memories; but I think it is seldom now that she feels its heaviness. Go out to her, Marcia my dear, and see if she seems troubled. She always has a welcome for the child," cousin Agnes added, as I unwillingly went away.

I found Lady Ferry in the garden; I stole my hand into hers, and, after a few minutes of silence, I was not surprised to hear her say that they had killed the Queen of France, poor Marie Antoinette! She had known her well in her childhood, before she was a queen at all—"A sad fate, a sad fate," said Lady Ferry. We went far down the gardens and by the river wall, and when we were again near the house, and could hear Mr McAllister's voice as cheery as ever, Madam took no notice of it. I had hoped she would go into the parlor again, and I wished over and over that I could have waited to hear the secrets which I was sure must have been told after cousin Agnes had sent me away.

One day I thought I had made a wonderful discovery. I was fond of reading, and found many books which interested me in cousin Matthew's fine library; but I took great pleasure also in hunting through a collection of old volumes which had been cast aside, either by him, or by some former owner of the house, and which were piled in a corner of the great garret. They were mostly yellow with age, and had dark brown leather or shabby paper bindings; the pictures in some were very amusing to me. I used often to find one which I appropriated and carried down stairs; and on this day I came upon a dusty, odd-shaped little book, for which I at once felt an affection. I looked at it a little. It seemed to be a journal, there were some stories of the Indians, and next I saw some reminiscences of the town of Boston, where, among other things, the author was told the marvellous story of one Mistress Honor Warburton, who was cursed, and doomed to live in this world forever. This was startling. I at once thought of Madam, and was reading on further to know the rest of the story, when someone called me, and I foolishly did not dare to carry my book with me. I was afraid I should not find it if I left it in sight; I saw an opening near me at the edge of the floor by the eaves, and I carefully laid my treasure inside. But, alas! I was not to be sure of its safe hiding place in a way that I fancied, for the book fell down between the boarding of the thick walls, and I heard it knock as it fell, and knew by the sound that it must be out of reach. I grieved over this loss for a long time; and I felt that it had been most unkindly taken out of my hand. I wished heartily that I could know the rest of the story; and I tried to summon courage to ask Madam, when we were by ourselves, if she had heard of Honor Warburton, but something held me back.

There were two other events just at this time which made this strange old friend of mine seem stranger than ever to me. I had a dream one night, which I took for a vision and a reality at the time. I thought I looked out of my window in the night, and there was bright moonlight, and I could see the other gable plainly; and I looked in at the windows of an unoccupied parlor which I never had seen open before, under Lady Ferry's own rooms. The shutters were pushed back, and there were candles burning; and I heard voices, and presently some tinkling music, like that of a harpsichord I had once heard in a very old house where I had been in England with my mother. I saw several couples go through with a slow, stately dance; and, when they stopped and seated themselves, I could hear their voices; but they spoke low, these midnight guests. I watched until the door was opened which led into the garden, and the company came out and stood for a few minutes on the little lawn, making their adieus, bowing low, and behaving with astonishing courtesy and elegance: finally the last goodnights were said, and they went away. Lady Ferry stood under the pointed porch, looking after them, and I could see her plainly in her brocade gown, with the impish flowers, a tall quaint cap, and a high lace frill at her throat, whiter than any lace I had ever seen, with a glitter on it; and there was a glitter on her face too. One of the other ladies was dressed in velvet, and I thought she looked beautiful: their eyes were all like sparks of fire. The gentlemen wore cloaks and ruffs, and high-peaked hats with wide brims, such as I had seen in some very old pictures which hung on the walls of the long west room. These were not pilgrims or Puritans, but gay gentlemen; and soon I heard the noise of their boats on the pebbles as they pushed off shore, and the splash of the oars in the water. Lady Ferry waved her hand, and went in at the door; and I found myself standing by the window in the chilly, cloudy night: the opposite gable, the garden, and the river, were indistinguishable in the darkness. I stole back to bed in an agony of fear; for it had been very real, that dream. I surely was at the window, for my hand had been on the sill when I waked; and I heard a church bell ring two o'clock in a town far up the river. I never had heard this solemn bell before, and it seemed frightful; but I knew afterward that in the silence of a misty night the sound of it came down along the water.

In the morning I found that there had been a gale in the night; and cousin Matthew said at breakfast time that the tide had risen so that it had carried off two old boats that had been left on the shore to go to pieces. I sprang to the window, and sure enough they had disappeared. I had played in one of them the day before. Should I tell cousin Matthew what I had seen or dreamed? But I was too sure that he would only laugh at me; and yet I was none the less sure that those boats had carried passengers.

When I went out to the garden, I hurried to the porch, and saw, to my disappointment, that there were great spiders' webs in the corners of the door, and around the latch, and that it had not been opened since I was there before. But I saw something shining in the grass, and found it was a silver knee buckle. It must have belonged to one of the ghostly guests, and my faith in them came back for a while, in spite of the cobwebs. By and by, I bravely carried it up to Madam, and asked if it were hers. Sometimes she would not answer for a long time, when one rudely broke in upon her reveries, and she hesitated now, looking at me with singular earnestness. Deborah was in the room; and, when she saw the buckle, she quietly said that it had been on the window ledge the day before, and must have slipped out. "I found it down by the doorstep in the grass," I said humbly; and then I offered Lady Ferry some strawberries which I had picked for her on a broad green leaf, and came away again.

A day or two after this, while my dream was still fresh in my mind, I went with Martha to her own home, which was a mile or two distant—a comfortable farmhouse for those days, where I was always made welcome. The servants were all very kind to me: as I recall it now, they seemed to have a pity for me, because I was the only child perhaps. I was very happy, that is certain, and I enjoyed my childish amusements as heartily as if there were no unfathomable mysteries or perplexities or sorrows anywhere in the world.

I was sitting by the fireplace at Martha's, and her grandmother, who was very old, and who was fast losing her wits, had been talking to me about Madam. I do not remember what she said, at least, it made little impression; but her grandson, a worthless fellow, sauntered in, and began to tell a story of his own, hearing of whom we spoke. "I was coming home late last night," said he, "and, as I was in that dark place along by the Noroway pines, old Lady Ferry she went by me, and I was near scared to death. She looked fearful tall—towered way up above me. Her face was all lit up with blue light, and her feet didn't touch the ground. She wasn't taking steps, she wasn't walking, but movin' along like a sailboat before the wind. I dodged behind some little birches, and I was scared she'd see me; but she went right out o' sight up the road. She ain't mortal."

"Don't scare the child with such foolishness," said his aunt disdainfully. "You'll be seein' worse things a-dancin' before your eyes than that poor, harmless old creatur' if you don't quit the ways you've been following lately. If that was last night, you were too drunk to see anything." And the fellow muttered, and went out, banging the door. But the story had been told, and I was stiffened and chilled with fright; and all the way home I was in terror, looking fearfully behind me again and again.

When I saw cousin Agnes, I felt safer, and since cousin Matthew was not at home, and we were alone, I could not resist telling her what I had heard. She listened to me kindly, and seemed so confident that my story was idle nonsense, that my fears were quieted. She talked to me until I no longer was a believer in there being any unhappy mystery or harmfulness; but I could not get over the fright, and I dreaded my lonely room, and I was glad enough when cousin Agnes, with her unfailing thoughtfulness, asked if I would like to have her come to sleep with me, and even went up stairs with me at my own early bedtime, saying that she should find it dull to sit all alone in the parlor. So I went to sleep, thinking of what I had heard, it is true, but no longer unhappy, because her dear arm was over me, and I was perfectly safe. I woke up for a little while in the night, and it was light in the room, so that I could see her face, fearless and sweet and sad, and I wondered, in my blessed sense of security, if she were ever afraid of anything, and why I myself had been afraid of Lady Ferry.

I will not tell other stories: they are much alike, all my memories of those weeks and months at the ferry, and I have no wish to be wearisome. The last time I saw Madam, she was standing in the garden door at dusk. I was going away before daylight in the morning. It was in the autumn: some dry leaves flittered about on the stone at her feet, and she was watching them. I said good-bye again, and she did not answer me; but I think she knew I was going away, and I am sure she was sorry, for we had been a great deal together; and, child as I was, I thought to how many friends she must have had to say farewell.

Although I wished to see my father and mother, I cried as if my heart would break because I had to leave the ferry. The time spent there had been the happiest time of all my life, I think. I was old enough to enjoy, but not to suffer much, and there was singularly little to trouble one. I did not know that my life was ever to be different. I have learned, since those childish days, that one must battle against storms if one would reach the calm which is to follow them. I have learned also that anxiety, sorrow, and regret fall to the lot of everyone, and that there is always underlying our lives, this mysterious and frightful element of existence; an uncertainty at times, though we do trust everything to God. Under the best loved and most beautiful face we know, there is hidden a skull as ghastly as that from which we turn aside with a shudder in the anatomist's cabinet. We smile, and are gay enough; God pity us! We try to forget our heartaches and remorse. We even call our lives commonplace, and, bearing our own heaviest burdens silently, we try to keep the commandment, and to bear one another's also. There is One who knows: we look forward, as He means we shall, and there is always a hand ready to help us, though we reach out for it doubtfully in the dark.

For many years after this summer was over, I lived in a distant, foreign country; at last my father and I were to go back to America. Cousin Agnes and cousin Matthew, and my mother, were all long since dead, and I rarely thought of my childhood, for in an eventful and hurried life the present claims one almost wholly. We were travelling in Europe, and it happened that one day I was in a bookshop in Amsterdam, waiting for an acquaintance whom I was to meet, and who was behind time.

The shop was a quaint place, and I amused myself by looking over an armful of old English books which a boy had thrown down near me, raising a cloud of dust which was plain evidence of their antiquity. I came to one, almost the last, which had a strangely familiar look, and I found that it was a copy of the same book which I had lost in the wall at the ferry. I bought it for a few coppers with the greatest satisfaction, and began at once to read it. It had been published in England early in the eighteenth century, and was written by one Mr Thomas Highward of Chester—a journal of his travels among some of the English colonists of North America, containing much curious and desirable knowledge, with some useful advice to those persons having intentions of emigrating. I looked at the prosy pages here and there, and finally found again those reminiscences of the town of Boston and the story of Mistress Honor Warburton, who was cursed, and doomed to live in this world to the end of time. She had lately been in Boston, but had disappeared again; she endeavored to disguise herself, and would not stay long in one place if she feared that her story was known, and that she was recognized. One Mr Fleming, a man of good standing and repute, and an officer of Her Majesty Queen Anne, had sworn to Mr Thomas Highward that his father, a person of great age, had once seen Mistress Warburton in his youth; that she then bore another name, but had the same appearance. "Not wishing to seem unduly credulous," said Mr Highward, "I disputed this tale; but there was some considerable evidence in its favour, and at least this woman was of vast age, and was spoken of with extreme wonder by the town's folk."

I could not help thinking of my old childish suspicions of Lady Ferry, though I smiled at the folly of them and of this story more than once. I tried to remember if I had heard of her death; but I was still a child when my cousin Agnes had died. Had poor Lady Ferry survived her? And what could have become of her? I asked my father, but he could remember nothing, if indeed he ever had heard of her death at all. He spoke of our cousins' kindness to this forlorn soul, and that, learning her desolation and her piteous history (and being the more pitiful because of her shattered mind), when she had last wandered to their door, they had cared for the old gentlewoman to the end of her days—"for I do not think she can be living yet," said my father, with a merry twinkle in his eyes: "she must have been nearly a hundred years old when you saw her. She belonged to a fine old family which had gone to wreck and ruin. She strayed about for years, and it was a godsend to her to have found such a home in her last days."

That same summer, we reached America, and for the first time since I had left it I went to the ferry. The house was still imposing, the prestige of the Haverford grandeur still lingered; but it looked forlorn and uncared for. It seemed very familiar; but the months I had spent there were so long ago, that they seemed almost to belong to another life. I sat alone on the doorstep for a long time, where I used often to watch for Lady Ferry; and forgotten thoughts and dreams of my childhood came back to me. The river was the only thing that seemed as young as ever. I looked in at some of the windows where the shutters were pushed back, and I walked about the garden, where I could hardly trace the walks, all over-grown with thick, short grass, though there were a few ragged lines of box, and some old rose bushes; and I saw the very last of the flowers—a bright red poppy, which had bloomed under a lilac tree among the weeds.

Out beyond the garden, on a slope by the river, I saw the family burying ground, and it was with a comfortable warmth at my heart that I stood inside the familiar old enclosure. There was my Lady Ferry's grave; there could be no mistake about it, and she was dead. I smiled at my satisfaction and at my foolish childish thoughts, and thanked God that there could be no truth in them, and that death comes surely—say, rather, that the better life comes surely—though it comes late.

The sad-looking, yellow-topped cypress, which only seems to feel quite at home in country burying grounds, had kindly spread itself like a coverlet over the grave, which already looked like a very old grave; and the headstone was leaning a little, not to be out of the fashion of the rest. I traced

again the words of old Colonel Haverford's pompous epitaph, and idly read some others. I remembered the old days so vividly there; I thought of my cousin Agnes, and wished that I could see her; and at last, as the daylight faded, I came away. When I crossed the river, the ferryman looked at me wonderingly, for my eyes were filled with tears. Although we were in shadow on the water, the last red glow of the sun blazed on the high gable windows, just as it did the first time I crossed over—only a child then, with my life before me.

I asked the ferryman some questions, but he could tell me nothing; he was a newcomer to that part of the country. He was sorry that the boat was not in better order; but there were almost never any passengers. The great house was out of repair: people would not live there, for they said it was haunted. Oh, yes! He had heard of Lady Ferry. She had lived to be very ancient; but she was dead.

"Yes," said I, "she is dead."

SARAH ORNE JEWETT · (1849–1909) was an American novelist, short story writer, and poet, known for her regional works set in Maine.